TELL ME A STORY, DADDY

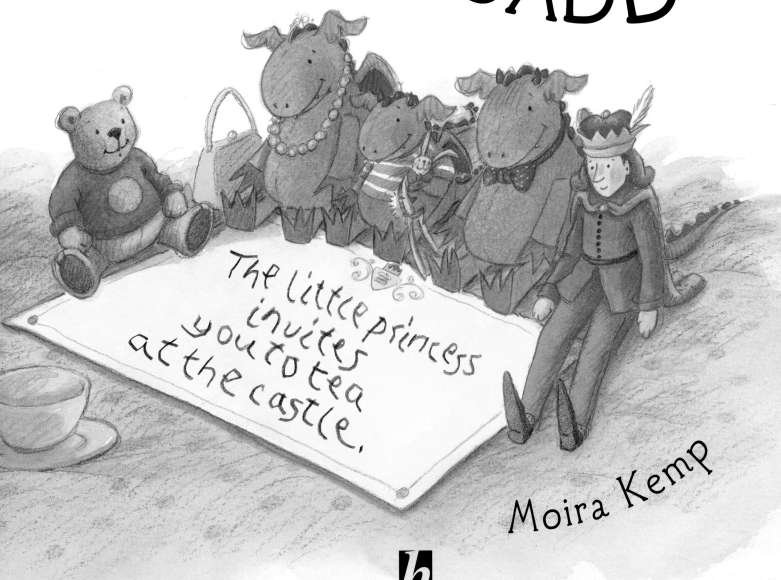

The little princess invites you to tea at the castle.

Moira Kemp

Hodder Children's Books

A division of Hodder Headline Limited

'Tell me a story, Daddy,'
said Rosie.
'Tell me a story about
a princess.'

For Deirdre, Dave, Peter and James.

British Library Cataloguing in Publication Data
A catalogue record of this book is available from the British Library.

ISBN 0 340 87559 3 HB
ISBN 0 340 87560 7 PB

Text and illustrations copyright © Moira Kemp 2005

The right of Moira Kemp to be identified as the author and
illustrator of this Work has been asserted by her in accordance
with the Copyright, Designs and Patents Act 1988.

10 9 8 7 6 5 4 3 2 1

First published 2005
by Hodder Children's Books,
a division of Hodder Headline Limited,
338 Euston Road, London, NW1 3BH

Printed in China

Daddy thought a bit and then he said, 'This is a story about
a little princess who lives in her very own castle.

One day she's having tea
with her teddy.

There are buns and biscuits, and
jellies and jam sandwiches, and iced
cakes and ice cream, and trifles and tarts
and teacakes, and lots and lots of fizzy lemonade.'

'But what if a hungry dragon wants to come for tea?'
said Rosie. 'Dragons are very greedy.'

And then she whispered, 'Teddy's a bit scared of dragons.'

'Well, he's not a
very big dragon,'
said Daddy.
'He's only a baby.'

'But what if his
mummy and daddy
come looking for him?'
said Rosie.
'They might be angry with
the little princess. They don't
know she's looking
after him.'

'Oh, she doesn't need to worry,' said Daddy. 'The bravest prince in the land is galloping to the castle to rescue her.'

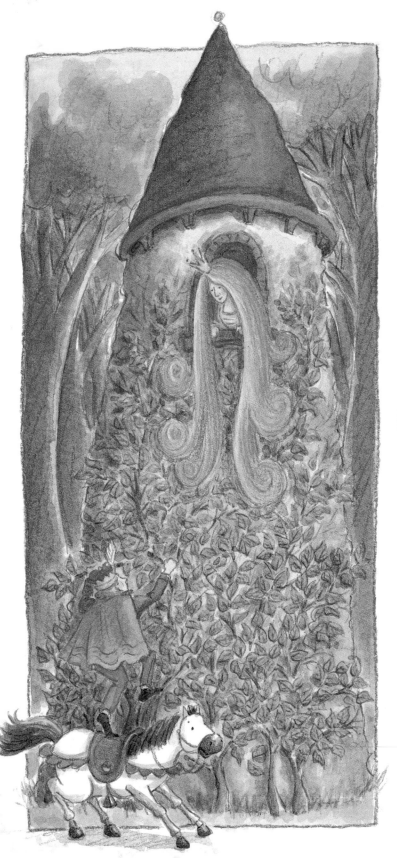

'But what if he has to rescue
another princess on the way?'
said Rosie. 'He might forget
all about the little princess
and her teddy.'

'He would never do that,' said Daddy.
'As soon as he's rescued the
princess, he jumps back
on his horse and gallops
to the castle as
fast as he can.'

'But what if the mummy and daddy
dragon get to the castle
before him?' said Rosie.

'They might roar at the little
princess. They might even
chase her and her teddy!'

'Not when they see the wonderful tea the baby dragon is having,' said Daddy. 'Especially the teacakes. Dragons can't resist teacakes.'

'But what if the dragons want to toast their teacakes?' said Rosie.
'They might set fire to the castle.'

'No, they won't,' said Daddy.
'The prince arrives just in time
and puts out the fire with
the fizzy lemonade.'

'The dragons
won't like that,'
warned Rosie.
'They'll be angry.'

'They'll feel better
when they've had some
more tea,' said Daddy.

'But there isn't any more tea!' wailed Rosie.
'The greedy baby dragon has gobbled
it all up. Every little bit.'

'Now the dragons are roaring.
They're chasing the little princess and if
they catch her they'll gobble her up –
and her teddy, too.'

'NO, THEY WON'T!' said Daddy. 'The little princess knows just what to do. She runs down to the kitchen as fast as she can.

And she SLAMS the door shut, to keep out those greedy dragons...

...until she's finished
making and baking...

...the gooiest, stickiest,
yummiest, scrummiest, most gobblesome
chocolate cake in the whole wide world.'

'And the
BIGGEST!'
laughed
Rosie.

'Then they eat **and eat**

and eat, said Daddy.

'And when they've gobbled it up, every little bit, the little princess tells them it's time to go to bed.'

'But they can't go to bed yet,' said Rosie.
'They're much too sticky. They have to
have a bath, first. And then they
have to put on their pyjamas.'

'Are they ready for bed, now?'
said Daddy.

'They can all go to bed,' said Rosie,
'when they've brushed their teeth.'

'The little princess tucks them all in and kisses them goodnight,' said Daddy.
'Does she tell them a bedtime story?' yawned Rosie.

'They're much too sleepy,' whispered Daddy.
'So she switches out the light and tiptoes very quietly out of the room…'

'Night, night,' murmured Rosie.

'…and before anyone can say
"Sweet Dreams", the little princess
and her teddy are fast asleep.'

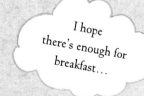

I hope
there's enough for
breakfast…